A Toy for Lulu

Written by
Michèle Dufresne

SO-AZX-852

PIONEER VALLEY EDUCATIONAL PRESS, INC.

Here is Lulu.
Lulu is a little puppy.

Here is Otis.
Otis is a big dog.

"I like to play!" said Lulu.
"I like to play with toys."

"Look," said Lulu.
"Here is a toy!
I will play
with this fun toy!"

"No!" said Otis.
"That is my toy."

"Look," said Lulu.
"Here is a toy!
I will play
with this fun toy!"

"No!" said Otis.
"That is my toy."

Lulu cried.
She cried and cried.

"Here is a toy," said Otis.
"You can play
with this toy."

"Thank you," said Lulu.
"I like this toy."